This is an Experiment

ALEXIS K. COGLEY

I dedicate this project to

my husband for always supporting my dreams,
my sons Maximus, Gabriel and Francis
for being my greatest teachers,
and myself.

table of contents

poems 5
musings. 46
wisdom 65

to you:

I hope somewhere along the way within these pages, you to find your way back to yourself – to your truth.
Our truth.

You are not powerless.

It's within your control to wake up and be an active designer of your reality. You are not, and never have been the victim — as you'll see, you're actually the hero!

Life is not happening to you.
Life is happening FOR you, because of you.

And now that you know this, it's time for you to take responsibility for your perception and your creative power.

There is nothing in this life you cannot do.
There is nothing in this life you cannot have.

And remember – *this is an experiment.*

I love you

poems

warning:
I have no shallow end
proceed with caution.

ALEXIS K COGLEY

I do everything with
intention and intensity.
apparently, it's a character flaw.

you know just how powerful you are.
why do you deny your Self?
give into it.

listen, baby.
it's all already waiting for you.
give into it.

it will be painful.
but momentary suffering vs eternal anguish?
give into it.

release those attachments given to you
by those who have loved & hurt.
give into it.

the Creator cannot be against you.
remember now.
give into it.

you've done this before.
been here before.
give into it.

being utterly lost and
being utterly found
feel very similar.

both send you swirling
through the depths
of this human experience
existing in only the breath.

here and not
all at once.

call it what you need but I've
seen beauty and I've tasted truth.
every thing is nothing – only energy.
I feel nothing – only pleasure even in the pain.
all but ignorance. so how could I ever return
when I search and I find it every time.
in every space, in every face.
Love is where my
soul dwells.

ALEXIS K COGLEY

I sometimes dream of being studied
by a lover or history scholars.

open me.
decipher me.

I beseech thee.

ALEXIS K COGLEY

POEMS

my soul moistens
at the thought of being
u n d e r s t o o d.

letting go of the shame
the sickening sinful feeling
the guilt I feel from simply being
h u m a n.

who has made me feel this way?
what trauma is responsible for the remorse that swells when
the breeze brushes my skin and sets me
a b l a z e.

these senses, they are sensitive.
aromas whisk me away,
twirling my mind like ramen around chopsticks.
fingertips thrill me.
accidental, sensual, or otherwise.
flavors cause my mouth to weep.
if I weren't a lady I'd surely
d r o o l.

beauty stuns me.
pulling at me so dangerously
that I'd wreck my own life just to look a little longer.
and music is pleasant but what of the whisper?
s w e e t e r.

only to be heard by the one.
just the thought of a stranger's warm breath falling on my neck
cracks me wide
o p e n.

it is said that my electricity can be
felt in the air like an approaching thunderstorm.
my smooth exhales and smoother words have been known
to caress necks and bend minds. my eyes so dark, so deep that
you'll yearn to be taken under. notice the way the warm wind
carries me. listen as the trees sing the song of my sigh and crack
your soul wide open. my tears have dissolved mountains.
everything graced by my earthly touch is left nurtured.
reborn and returned to truth.

I hear what I should hear
and see what I should be seeing.
what we all should.
it is all around and in us.
flowing, dancing, harmonizing you with me.
and *they* with *we*.
as light each color at once.
open your eye and see Her
reach out to Her and let Her touch you.
show you.

ALEXIS K COGLEY

listen more
do less.
learn from nature
to take care
but don't obsess.

there was a call
I'd been long ignoring.
so the other day
I went out exploring.
it led me to a
mesmerizing place.
clouds of gold, honey rain
and your face.
I walked slowly and soon
I began to run.
it felt like coming home
exposing my soul to the sun.
floating and swirling
free from thats and thisses.
there were stars in my eyes
and on my lips,
butterfly kisses.

ALEXIS K COGLEY

every moment is fleeting
which makes the one we're
in so fucking magic.
to have it, then to not
is what keeps us seeking
it's what keeps us
finding.

POEMS

she said,
*I want to sit on a rock and have you dance
for me in the sunshine.*

and i turned on.

she said,
*I'm so attracted to your mind,
I want to know your every thought.*

and i spilled over.

she said,
*You have me walking on the moon.
I feel weightless and limitless.*

and we floated.

she said,
*I like watching you and
taking in every detail.*

and i felt seen.

she said,
Let's be one in one another.

and i fell.

she said,
I want to whisper life into you.

and I died.

ALEXIS K COGLEY

can you
look at me in the eyes;
admire the way my
mind and heart wander;
study the language
of my body and tongue;
worship me?

it was a simultaneous
swell and release.

making love to a thunderstorm
ain't for the weak.

the more intensely I began to feel,
the heavier the rain fell.

and the wetter I got.
trembling there

with lightning behind my eyes, and
puddles between my thighs.

ALEXIS K COGLEY

come swim at the waterfall of my thoughts
bathe in all my dreams and guarded secrets
quench yourself in my wildest desires
and when you've had your fill
leave me

– empty and exhausted.

you are here
I am there
smoldering
in the embers
of taboo desire.
slipping into
restlessness
until the inferno
ignites again
in an instant
with a word
a breath
a thought
on my skin
in my mouth
through my soul.
you are here
seducing me
inducing soaked sheets.
i am there
the shallow inhale
in your belly.

ALEXIS K COGLEY

drooling lips
and pulsing hips
dreaming of your
lightning fingertips.

i wish i could sleep.
i wish i could hear you.
i wish i could eat.
i wish i could hold you.
i wish i could settle.
i wish i could kiss you.
i wish i could breathe.
i wish i could ease you.

i hope that you rest.
i hope that you miss me.
i hope that you smile.
i hope that you call me.
i hope that you paint.
i hope that you want me.
i hope that you find peace.

ALEXIS K COGLEY

may we dampen our selves
in the mist of the divine frequently
until the ego is soggy, weighted and
altogether forgone.

my body lay hopeless as
her gaze rips me from sleep
and tosses me out to sea.
holding me as if with intent
under vexing waves of desire
yet again.

what could be said of the heat
passing through me?
feverishly puzzling how to go
deeper with her without drowning.
she haunts, taunts and tempts me
with that damn smile.
and that wild look she gives when
she is feeling it too.

here only palpitating thuds
against my rib cage and
moans and heavy sighs escaping
with each quiver of my lips
only to be heard by the twisted
sheets in my fists.

ALEXIS K COGLEY

i'm lusting
or your attention
for your mouth.
fuck

just saying
your name
gets me high
and fervent.

your breath
on my neck
splits my soul right
down the middle.

the wetness of
your tongue
on my lips
tempers my ocean.

i want you
so fucking badly
i writhe
in torturous ecstasy

– *lusting.*

I'm almost certain
it was all just my imagination.
it had to be a figment, right?
you were never here with me.

because there's no way I exposed
myself to you like that.
there's no way I filled my belly
with your words, your fantasies.

tell me that I was dreaming,
tell me that I'm overthinking,
tell me I'm childlike and naive.
tell me it was all just my imagination.

there's no way we...

there's just no fucking way.

ALEXIS K COGLEY

can we just skip to the part
where we laugh about this as homies?
to the part where your silence doesn't
utterly destroy me.

when you spoke it was like you knew me.
you painted fantasies in my mind and on my heart.
i told you i couldn't understand this
you said *twin flames.*
i told you i was scared, you said *trust me.*
you declared *I only want to bring peace to you*
then you disappeared.

holy shit,
I've been love bombed

ALEXIS K COGLEY

I only wanted
to move through
my heart's doorway
into a deeper space
of Love.

to flow
and merge
with a soul like yours
into Oneness.

to experience the preciousness
the grace, the sweetness
of you – of God.

to move beyond
the relations of
our human condition.

to feel at home
in that Oneness.
where we are never afraid
to be in Love.

that's all I wanted.

POEMS

I talked to you last night.
chattering away in the kitchen,
dancing and spilling wine.

you sat stuck on my sofa
in a way that allowed only for
a gaze – that gaze, *your* gaze.

and I said everything.
all of my love and sadness for you
left in cold puddles on the floor.

I danced for you last night, again,
ignoring the hazard of slipping, again
. . .falling, again.

and you just stared
and I just laughed
because you weren't there.

I was talking to and dancing with
and falling for an illusion –
a beautiful, convincing hallucination.

my sofa vacant,
my glass empty, and
the song in my heart silenced.

ALEXIS K COGLEY

Love doesn't suck
that person sucks.

and even they don't suck
their actions fucking suck.

POEMS

for a moment, I had it all figured out
all the answers
the only answer, even
I knew *why*

as clearly as I see my hands before me now
perhaps even clearer
I saw the journey and the destination
each path and it's result

existing in both night and day
I was above it all. I had done it all
conquered all
I was solid gold; but greater

maybe a star, a celestial being
permeating with creative and destructive
time could not escape me
light envied me

the entire universe, in me
magic here, within my warmth
wisdom so profound
I was forced to awaken

forced to forget.

ALEXIS K COGLEY

what is it
about beauty that
stuns me?
why can I feel it
in the base of
my heart?
one hard thump
behind my ribs.
there's a pain at
first sight.
an aching urge
to bow down to it.
instead,
I cry.

POEMS

I wonder
is the light of the Sun
as arousing to you
as it is to me?

like his heat was made
for my skin alone.
and I melt
every time.

do you also breathe out
a small moan
when he touches
you?

ALEXIS K COGLEY

you are
so divine
i can practically
see the stars
falling from your
dazzling skin

where do you go when you're hiding
from the world – from me?

did you know that even when you go
I can feel you still, hear you still?

there's no space in which you can retreat
dark enough that I cannot see you.

no depth to which you can descend
deep or cold enough that I cannot love you.

nor time that can pass long enough
that I cannot remember you.

ALEXIS K COGLEY

I do not know which is better.
is it the way he holds my shadow in every way I've ever wanted from anyone; or is it the way he makes me cum without ever touching me? thank God I do not have to choose between the two.

seductive and divine
all at the same damn time
sweeter than summer
grapes straight off the vine
come splash in the puddles
of a mind like mine
I promise you'll be thrilled
by what you find

ALEXIS K COGLEY

does it make you paranoid
that I want nothing from you?
has the ground beneath your feet
turned to air now that you realize
I only come to spill into you?

POEMS

the only enemy
to ever exist
is hiding
in the last place
many of us
think to look

– within.

ALEXIS K COGLEY

what was
once a
prison
I've transformed
into a
p o r t a l.

I warned you.
I have no shallow end
but you jumped in anyway.

You drowned in me.
that's on you
I'm not even a little sorry.

musings

MUSINGS

There is no
distance you cannot
return from. No deed you can do,
thought you could have, nor word you can speak
that could deny you entry
into Love.

ALEXIS K COGLEY

Life will always be short for those who
don't live in the present moment.

Don't mistake subtly for insignificance.

Slow down, give your attention. Intention.
With a little attention to detail, everything becomes a romance.

MUSINGS

Smiled at myself from within myself this morning. I can't remember the last time I did, or if I even have before. But I liked it. I liked me, I liked what and who I saw. Noticing past the form for once, though my sparkling eyes straight into my own soul. I felt love for me. I felt gentleness and mercy and pride. I recognized myself, I knew myself.

A fresh bud, finally blooming after all the rain and days of sun far too hot to open. And I'm beautiful.

ALEXIS K COGLEY

We d e l a y our evolution

when we r e s i s t our experience.

Surrender and flow truly are the only way to thrive.

MUSINGS

What if death is not negative.
Consider it is not darkness, nor maleficence.

What if death is neutral. What if it is *safe*.
The light between birth and birth.

Indeed, death is part of the process.
Not an end, but a continuation.

ALEXIS K COGLEY

You know that feeling when you're squirming and itching to be free from your own body, your own human existence; when you're desperately getting high just to get a different perspective; when you're painfully yearning to (re)connect or tap into something meaningful, something loving; when you're driving your head into the pillow in the middle of the day, begging for sleep so you can escape the weight of awakeness; when you're walking in place for miles lost in resentful prayer and pleading for release, for understanding. . .

No. . ?

Me neither.

MUSINGS

I've been a liar and I've been a cheat.
I lost relationships because of it.

Now I am open and honest.
I lose relationships because of it.

Understand there is no right way.

ALEXIS K COGLEY

I've given it all up. Not through pressure, but through surrender. Through grace. I don't presume to know anything at all. I do only what feels right, what feels inspired and nothing else. I am no longer convinced, nor can I be further conditioned against my will. I declare myself completely free from the illusion of lack and limitation. I declare that harmony and peace of mind reign supreme in my life and in my mind – forever more. I embody outer beauty and inner perfection, as I was made to. I am lifted in consciousness, rooted in truth. I am in my true place at all times.

MUSINGS

I've spent a lot of time watching myself, watching my sisters and my brothers and the animals. And I've come to understand something:

WE ARE —

the order and the chaos.
the doer and the happening.
the harmony and the discord.
the seeker and that which is sought.
the peaceful center,

— Suns of God.

"What a waste of time".

Funny little saying.
Can we? Waste time.

Can we even "use it wisely"?

No moment can be wasted. Even in the moments when we're doing nothing. Seemingly being nothing, with no desire or motivation. There we still learn about ourselves. Something is still being revealed. Details still being handled beyond sight and sense. Evolving in micro, but no less important, ways.

So relax. You are not wasting your time.
You can't.

MUSINGS

Maybe you should QUIT.

Quit giving up on yourself.

Quit talking and overthinking yourself out of greatness.

Quit pretending like you aren't wonderfully capable of creating the reality of your dreams – just as you are right now!

Who you *think* you are is vulnerable and afraid. Who you *actually* are is well-protected, abundantly resourced, and brave.

You have to intentionally and fearlessly change the way you understand yourself.

Take off and throw away the limited, low-quality lenses given to you, and choose to see things from a true point of view.

Then you'll realize you're exceedingly more capable than you've been conditioned to believe.

ALEXIS K COGLEY

You are connected to your wholeness, to your worthiness in every moment. You live in a true and loving way, towards yourself and towards others. You are an empowered designer and co-creator of this human experience. You are expansive and limitless. Open yourself to creative and intuitive solutions for peace and abundance. Your existence is one of aligned magnificence.

MUSINGS

Practice being inaccessible.
Just completely unavailable – on purpose.

A very dear friend of mine, she asked me
"how do you manage to find time for yourself?"

I told her: "I don't.
I don't find time – I TAKE it."
I demand it, actually.

The difference is intention.
The difference is I give myself permission.
The difference is *authority*.

If you're looking for time, you'll forever be looking.

Make time. Take time.
It's the only way you can be any good to the people you love, the people who count on you.

It's the only way you can be any good for YOU.

Time and energy are sacred resources, and it serves everyone when you serve yourSelf... *first*.

ABUNDANCE SHORTCUT

Step 1: Notice the abundance already in your life.
Step 2: Express gratitude in everything you do.
Step 3: Watch how things multiply!
Step 4: Repeat

MUSINGS

I've stopped believing in hard work.
No more following formulas or restricting myself – in any area of Life. I now believe in conscious and intentional action, habitual aligned thinking, positive anticipation, and faith so fierce that everything I want has no fucking choice but to *find me.*

I've also given up believing in sacrifice or compromise.
Instead, I believe in having this AND that. I trust (and EXPECT) that when I am crystal clear on what I want my life to look, feel, smell, taste and sound like. . .submit my desires to the Source of all creativity. . .stop obsessing over the "how". . .and consciously choose to accept nothing less than what vibrationally matches my desires. . .it will be delivered to me.

I no longer believe in set-backs.
Everything is forward motion. It's all in my favor! No more setting goals or having a strategy. When I commit to the life I want and begin to move in alignment, the way will present itself to me and always provide what I need as I need it.

Fuck being "realistic". I can't even comprehend what that's supposed to mean. I am the designer of MY reality. And the Creator honors my right to create. So who is anyone else outside of myself to tell me what is "realistic" for me!?

There was this time when I was twenty-five on an international flight to Greece. Even as we were suspended somewhere over the Atlantic, I couldn't believe it was a real experience I was having. Every detail felt like a vivid dream. But there I was at 8:18PM, in and out of sleep as the plane was in and out of turbulence.

God heard my prayers.

I was sharing the A/B seats of the 28th row with one of my class mates. We agreed to take turns sitting in the window seat. When it was my turn, the sun had long set. I didn't expect to see much. Yet God amazed me - as She often does.

The stars! Oh. My. Gosh! The stars!! I almost couldn't comprehend what I was looking at. I don't think I had ever seen anything so beautiful or awe-inspiring since the birth of my son. I felt blessed. I felt overwhelmed. I felt undeserving. But more than anything else, I felt special as I had a realization:

> The same God that created the heavens, created me. That divine intelligence dwells within. Just as She has carefully placed each star in its place, so has She placed me in this world. I am a masterpiece. A part of The Master Plan. I am Her design. She is my creator!

And I. Am. So. Beautiful.

MUSINGS

I often dream that I am somewhere nobody even knows me. I introduce myself with syllables of truth and certainty. I depend on no one. Tied to no one. Attached to no thing. Yet still very deeply interconnected to all and every. Maybe in a modest apartment. Perfectly white, jasmine-scented sheets – draped over a bed only I sleep in. No one demanding on my time. No thing siphoning my energy. Sacred resources spent on loving myself selfishly. Attracting passion from all living things like a magnet. The laws of the land don't apply here.

I love who I want. Or no one at all. The choice is entirely mine. And those who love and have loved me understand my words when I speak. They comprehend my madness. They set me free, knowing I will return.

Tomorrow. Or next year. Or next lifetime.

How can I fault you for not recognizing Love when I came through your door? For excusing me as lust and with intellect.

I was denied from the position of human understanding. So I get it. You may have never seen Love before.

How could you recognize me? You do not even recognize your Self. I do not fault you for your unreadiness. But Love I still am, and love you I still do.

wisdom

ALEXIS K COGLEY

There is order and there is chaos in this life.
And You are at the center – the peaceful center.
What is outside of you cannot penetrate you.
For You are unreachable, but never separate.

And so it is!

WISDOM GAINED

This is your curriculum.
What you are experiencing is not an error.
The place you're in is the right one.
This is it. Perfect because it is. Perfect as it has always been.

ALEXIS K COGLEY

Your body and your mind are your only instruments;
it is essential that you calibrate, stabilize, and healthily maintain your instruments.

WISDOM GAINED

You're not crazy, you're *intuitive*.

Learn to trust our own intelligence and the feedback that's coming from inside.

ALEXIS K COGLEY

It's extremely important, especially in the morning, to **be quiet**.

WISDOM GAINED

Good or bad,
we always find what we're looking for.

The Universe will bless you, and humble you.
Accept both thankfully.

WISDOM GAINED

Your *entire reality* is based on your words, thoughts and beliefs. You should be obsessed with getting them into alignment with your dreams!

Meditation is the foundation of all manifestation.

Meditate in the darkness, just before you fall to sleep. Envision your ideal reality. Bring every single detail into existence in your imagination.

Then lay your head down, but keep conjuring. Really sink into it.
The emotion of it, the smells, the sounds, even the taste and textures.

Once you have it, set it free. Your imagination is your commandment. As you drift, your subconscious mind and God will take from there – conspiring on your behalf and twisting matter into your every desire.

While you sleep. . .

WISDOM GAINED

Keeping your word to yourself is the highest form of self Love and respect.

ALEXIS K COGLEY

Relish every single part of the journey –
especially when it's nothing like you planned.

Letting go of control is how we gain control.

ALEXIS K COGLEY

Resistance is no good.
Let the sandpaper of Life
soften and smooth your soul.

WISDOM GAINED

WARNING:

idealistic notions of Love
may potentially harm
the subject of said notions
and will most certainly destroy
the originator.

The more frequently you say you can't,
the more consistently you will not be able to. And vice versa.

Think of your default words and thoughts and beliefs as code, and your subconscious mind as a computer.

You are coding with your words, thoughts and beliefs. And your subconscious mind, as the obedient computer, will carry out whatever it is given.

So – and I stress this – *code accordingly.*

WISDOM GAINED

When your hunger for truth begins to outweigh your ego's clutch onto self-reinforcing suffering and illusion. . .then you will start to understand that discomfort is essential to evolution. Disappointment, fear anger, judgement – these are all your teachers. Only mirrors reflecting where you're still clutching.

Listen to me carefully: Stop trying to hide your darkness, pretending it's not there.

You need it! It is a deep well from which you can draw significant power. Not to mention, it makes you so fucking beautiful.

Let me tell you what you get when you suppress the darkness –

    not knowing who you really are, because you're trying to exist as half of you.
    no idea what makes you feel joy, because you avoid feeling sorrow.
    devoid of creativity, because you cut yourself off from Life's richest inspiration.
    allowing other's labels to define you, their fickle judgments sway you, and their small minds cage you.

The list of detriments goes on...the choice is, as it has always been, yours.

WISDOM GAINED

The only thing in your way... is you.
So move.
Move. And guess what – God will move with you.

Do you understand what that means?
To have God be moving with you.
To have The Universe conspiring for you, designing for you!

Graciously transforming any obstacle into a beautiful lesson so that you may be smarter, stronger, softer, quicker, more aligned, and more loving for all that is in store for you.

Like, what can't you do?
What can't you have?
What level can't you reach?!

The Universe wants to give.
The Universe in all its abundance cannot help but to give to you. But you first have to put down the shit that you carry, shit that means nothing other than the meaning you give it by holding on.

Put it down and make space.

You don't need some physical sacred space. *YOU are the sacred space*. The peace is within you. You can bless any space and make it sacred. It's literally you, and has forever been.

You are a creator. Co-creating with the One and the Only Divine Source. That is how powerful you are.
Not some weak and confused being too crippled to move.

You cannot fail.

Take yourself seriously.
Scratch that.

Take yourself *SACREDLY*.

And take no shit.

WISDOM GAINED

Observe how you talk to yourself.

Your inner warrior is ALWAYS listening.
She will carry out any command she is given.
Faithfully.

Your word is too fucking powerful for you to be reckless with it.

You are in possession of a powerful force. The force of choice.
It led you here. To these words.
Your capacity to choose is your greatest strength. Your words, your thoughts and your beliefs are you tools for manifestation. Your wand, if you will.

Wield them in creation of goodness, health and abundance.
Prayer, meditation, affirmations...Whatever you call it, your words and your choices are powerful, with the ability to literally create or destroy.

How's the saying go?
"The tongue is mightier than the sword."
You were and are never out of control. You've only been convinced that you were/are.
Use you're words and your thoughts to take your power back!

You are not a victim.
Create, change and delete as you see fit.

WISDOM GAINED

I'm here to tell you that it's okay to be yourself now. You can shed that false identity. It's okay to stop pretending to be, and just be. It's okay for you to stop only appearing to be, and just be. The only one judging you, is you. It's okay to let go of that now. I can tell you from firsthand experience that when you do. . . everything begins to shift. You will realize that The Universe is responsive in nature, and will respond to your faith in a big way.

Pause and check in with yourself right now. Is your nervous system ramping up? That's okay. That's a good sign.

It means you're moving into the unknown. It means your ego is trembling and pleading for its old, familiar bullshit. But you're moving on. You're moving up!

To a place where the old, stale, limited narrative cannot go. I know it feels a little scary. But I'm here to tell you that it's okay.

Peace is not something that can be found.

It's a state of being that is created – from within.

It is a choice to be made as moments give way to moments.

Peace is the intentional creation of space for all good things like Love and Joy to dwell and coexist with the fullness of our humanity, *without trying to change it.*

WISDOM GAINED

In order to transcend sadness, you must acknowledge and embrace it. Just by sitting with your pain, you are actively allowing release. One of the strongest things you can do is fully feel the emotions you're experiencing.

It's not about avoiding the dark and moving toward the light. The amount of light that we can bring to the world is equal to the amount of darkness the we can accept and love within ourselves.

Where sadness was my teacher,
Love is now my guide.

It starts with a thought. Then another one. And then a few more.

Until the infinite intelligence within you and Divine Source are in alignment, conspiring on behalf of your boldest dreams. Your superpower is your thought, your conviction. You have the ability to manipulate, bend, destroy and create reality as you see fit. The mind serves you, not the other way around.

Inhale, envision it. Exhale, command it.

WISDOM GAINED

Sometimes you'll encounter and experience some of the most beautiful, bewitching things on this planet. Things that clutch tight onto your soul without ever coming near you. Things that transcend earthly emotion. Beings and phenomena alike will set you ablaze and leave you smoldering and unsatisfied.

And believe me, you will be inclined to touch and intertwine with these things – to feel the electricity at your fingertips, on your lips and inside your veins. To inhale their sweet and sticky floating vapors deep down into the basement of your lungs.

But you must'nt, because if you do. . .you'll certainly ruin it. Ruin you. So just stand there – tingling and mystified. On fire with eternal longing.

To my inner child –

I would hold her, the way she was never held.
I would see here and instantly feel it all again.
The shame, the pain, the betrayal, the wishing for death.
Upon contact, I'd be compelled to gently ring out her tear-soaked soul. Because I know intimately the weight it bears.
Just as I know I cannot change a thing. I cannot spare her the trauma or internal torment.
It was all necessary.
Excruciating, confusing, isolating – but so necessary.

I could only offer assurances, "it gets betters".
She'd have to look at me, really see me, to understand that it didn't kill us.
None of it. Weary, maybe. But not dead.
"It's going to be really fucking hard, baby.
And it will hurt some more. But we are one hell of a fucking Woman…"

WISDOM GAINED

Love leaves us naked, gooey from the womb and commands with its truth the death of all insecurity without so much as a whisper.

Fear must slink down our soft shoulders and drip from our fresh fingertips, dissolving into the nothingness from which it conjured masterful and desperate illusions.

When you've seen the bodiless you, you can no longer be deceived by your flesh or your ego.

You then understand that you are formless perfection.

WISDOM GAINED

Delight in the whole experience
and learn everything you can.
It's all happening for your ascension,
as part of the Divine Plan.

*It's been an honor and a pleasure
to share myself with you.*

Thank you.

Made in the USA
Middletown, DE
13 May 2024

54259142R00057